Pets RULE!

Invasion of
the Pugs

Read all the **Pets RULE!** books

1 Pets RULE! My Kingdom of Darkness
Written by Susan Tan
Illustrated by Wendy Tan Shiau Wei
SCHOLASTIC

2 Pets RULE! The Poodle of Doom
Written by Susan Tan
Illustrated by Wendy Tan Shiau Wei
SCHOLASTIC

3 Pets RULE! Kittens Are Monsters
Written by Susan Tan
Illustrated by Wendy Tan Shiau Wei
SCHOLASTIC

4 Pets RULE! The Rise of The Goldfish
Written by Susan Tan
Illustrated by Wendy Tan Shiau Wei
SCHOLASTIC

5 Pets RULE! Invasion of the Pugs
Written by Susan Tan
Illustrated by Wendy Tan Shiau Wei
SCHOLASTIC

6 Pets RULE! The Night of the Chipmunk
Written by Susan Tan
Illustrated by Wendy Tan Shiau Wei
SCHOLASTIC

Invasion of the Pugs

Written by
Susan Tan

Illustrated by
Wendy Tan Shiau Wei

BRANCHES

SCHOLASTIC INC.

To Maisie, pug of my heart – ST

To Lucky, my sweetest baby in the world! – WTSW

Text copyright © 2024 by Susan Tan
Illustrations copyright © 2024 by Wendy Tan Shiau Wei

Library of Congress Cataloging-in-Publication Data

Names: Tan, Susan, author. | Wei, Wendy Tan Shiau, illustrator. | Tan, Susan. Pets rule ; 5.
Title: Invasion of the pugs / by Susan Tan ; illustrated by Wendy Tan Shiau Wei.
Description: First edition. | New York : Branches/Scholastic, 2024. | Series: Pets rule! ; 5 |
Audience: Ages 6-8. | Audience: Grades 2-3. |
Summary: It is hard for Chihuahua Ember to decide which is worse: a pack of pugs who announce that they are aliens, or the dog park which is filled with large and overexcited dogs--but he is convinced that he and his animal friends must stop the pugs to save the world (for themselves).
Identifiers: LCCN 2023019110 | ISBN 9781339021577 (paperback) | ISBN 9781339021584 (library binding) | ISBN 9781339021591 (ebook)
Subjects: LCSH: Chihuahua (Dog breed—Juvenile fiction. | Pug—Juvenile fiction. | Dogs—Juvenile fiction. | Animals—Juvenile fiction. | Park for dogs—Juvenile fiction. | Humorous stories. |
CYAC: Chihuahuas (Dog breeds—Fiction. | Pug—Fiction. | Dogs—Fiction. | Animals—Fiction. |
Parks for dogs—Fiction. | Humorous stories. | BISAC: JUVENILE FICTION / Readers / Chapter Books |
JUVENILE FICTION / People & Places / United States / Asian American & Pacific Islander |
LCGFT: Animal fiction. | Humorous fiction.
Classification: LCC PZ7.1.T37 In 2024 | DDC 813.6 [Fic]—dc23/eng/20230613
LC record available at https://lccn.loc.gov/2023019110

10 9 8 7 6 5 4 3 2 1   24 25 26 27

Printed in India   197
First edition, April 2024
Edited by Cindy Kim
Cover design by Brian LaRossa
Book design by Jaime Lucero

Table of Contents

Kevin

Mr. Chin

Neo

Mrs. Chin

The Chin Family

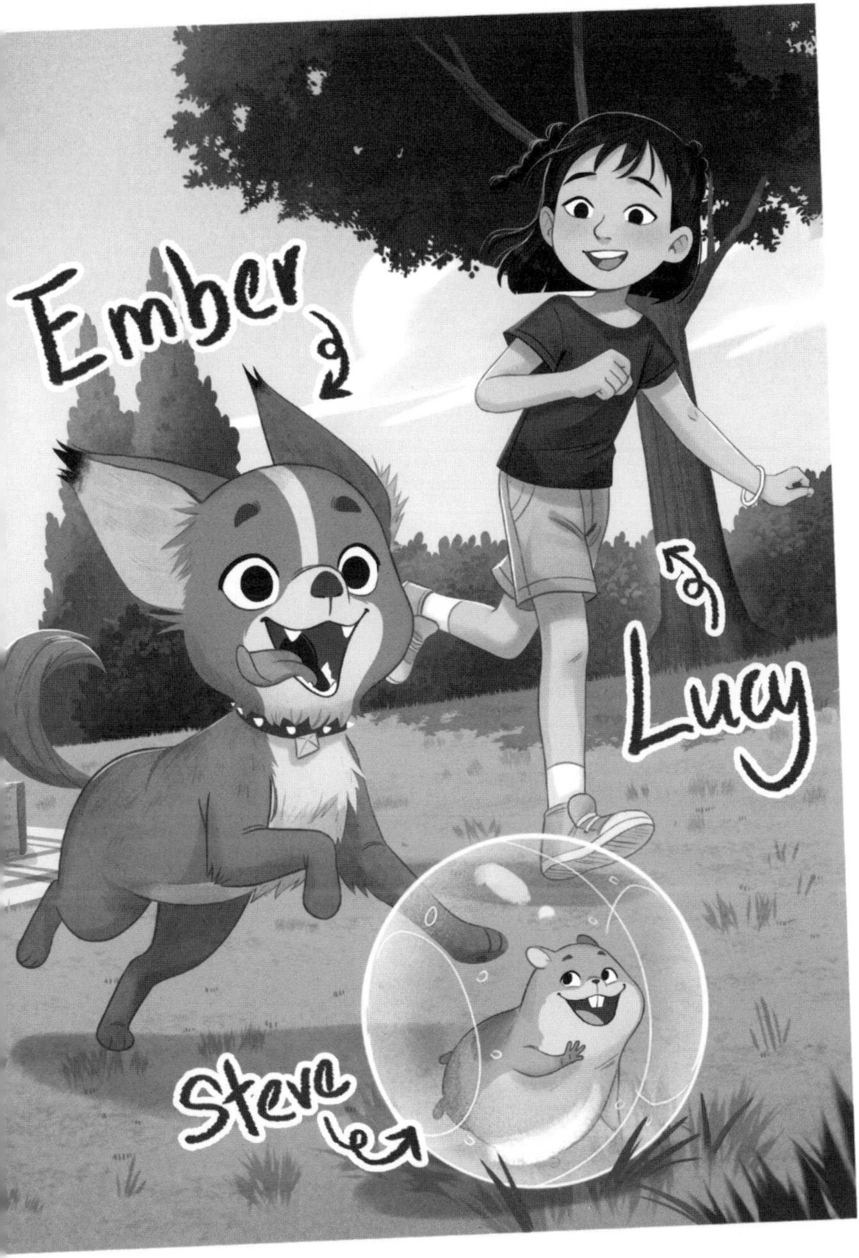
Ember
Lucy
Steve

CHAPTER 1

Evil Wears Curly Tails

I stood on the porch steps. I couldn't believe my eyes. Out in the front yard were the strangest dogs I'd ever seen. They were being walked by a human I didn't know.

"Take us to your leader," the pugs said. Their voices sounded strange and almost scary. "Soon your planet will be ours!"

I gasped. The pugs had an evil plan! I am Ember the mighty, future ruler of this world, and if anyone is going to rule the planet, it is going to be *me*.

"This is Kai, the dog walker," Mr. Chin explained to Lucy and Kevin. "Kai is going to take Ember to a doggy-playtime group at the park every day. The pugs live down the road, and they started going there earlier this week. Now, they can all walk there together. It's the perfect summer plan!"

"No, that's a TERRIBLE plan. I should be at home with Steve and Neo! I forbid it!" I said.

But as usual, Mr. Chin didn't listen.

"Come say hello, Ember," he said.

I didn't want to say hello or go to the dog park. But all the humans were looking at me. So I crept down the porch steps.

When I got to the bottom, one pug was sniffing the pavement. Another was nibbling the grass.

The pugs had curly tails and giant eyes. I sniffed one of them. She smelled like a normal dog. But maybe this was a part of their evil disguise.

I knew I had to show the pugs that I was the boss. So I puffed out my chest and stood as tall as I could.

"Hello," I said to the smallest pug. "I am Ember, future ruler of this world."

"Greetings," she said. By itself, her voice didn't sound scary. But then she went on. "It's nice to meet you, Earthling. Soon this place will be ours."

My fur stood on end. "Earthling" means a creature from Earth. So, did the pugs come from . . . another planet?

"Wait," I gasped. "If I'm an Earthling, you must all be . . . aliens!"

"You're smarter than you look. But you cannot stop us," she replied.

Just then, Mr. Chin and Kai walked over.

"I'm glad you came, Kai. Ember is making new friends already!" Mr. Chin said.

"These dogs are NOT friends! They're plotting to take over the earth!" I barked at Mr. Chin.

"Aw, don't worry, Ember, you'll see them tomorrow," Mr. Chin said.

I barked at him again, annoyed that he didn't understand.

"Come on, guys!" Kai said, guiding the pugs away.

But before they left, the pugs all turned and stared at me.

"Stay out of our way, Earthling," they whispered. "Or you'll be sorry!"

CHAPTER 2

I (Don't) Want to Believe

I followed my humans inside. I ran to find Smelly Steve the hamster and Neo the canary, two other Chin family pets. Then I told them what happened.

"No way!" Steve gasped.

"Aliens are real?!" Neo asked.

"We need to stop their evil plans," I said.

"If only BeBe were here, too," Neo said. "She's a brave action-hero kind of bug." But BeBe was away visiting her friend, Ari the spider.

We all nodded as Lucy came into the hall.

"Hey, Chin pets! We're having a movie night!" Lucy said, holding a plate of pizza.

"Oh yay!" Steve said happily. On movie nights, the Chins eat dinner in the living room.

I settled on the couch and got excited . . . until the movie began.

It turned out that the movie was about aliens!

My fur stood up. There were laser beams and epic space battles.

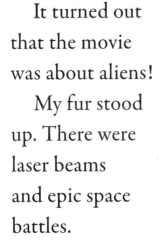

Oh no! Is this the kind of alien takeover the pugs were planning?

By the end, I was hiding under the couch with Steve and Neo.

"That movie was TERRIBLE," Steve said.

"I was so scared," Neo agreed.

"Me too," I said quietly. Thanks to my friends, I've learned that, sometimes, it's okay to admit when you're scared. "We'll figure something out."

But none of us could stop thinking about the movie. It was still on my mind as Lucy and I got ready for bed.

"Tomorrow will be a great day," Lucy said as she got under the covers. "It's the first day of swim camp! Lia and Arjun will be there, too!"

"You will have the best summer ever. I command it!" I said. "With no aliens allowed!"

I put my nose in her ear and she giggled.

As I curled up on Lucy's pillow, I thought about the next day.

We *had* to stop the pugs! But how?

I did NOT want to go to the park to meet strange new dogs, either. The thought made my stomach flip.

I wanted to stay at home with my friends. I knew the pugs wouldn't stand a chance against us, if we only had time to plot against them.

That was it! I bolted up on the pillow.

I could avoid the dog park AND save the world!

And I knew just what to do.

CHAPTER 3

Hide and Smell

The next morning, Lucy got ready for camp and went downstairs for breakfast. Usually, I sit by her chair and she feeds me pieces of toast. But today, I ran to Mr. Chin's study instead.

Mr. Chin has lots of sculptures in his office. This means there are LOTS of places to hide.

I burst into the room.

"Bubbles!" I called. Bubbles is the Chins' pet goldfish. She used to want to rule the world, but she changed her mind once she got a new friend. Now she lives in her tank with a red fish named Boba.

"Help—you have to hide me!" I told Bubbles and Boba. "I don't want to go to the dog park!"

"Have you ever been there before?" Boba asked.

"No, but I don't need to be around other dogs," I said. "I have plenty of friends!"

"But, Ember, you will make *new* friends there. It could be fun!" Bubbles said. "Making friends was exactly what *I* needed."

"I don't need new friends!" I insisted.

Suddenly, I heard the door open.

"Ember, Mr. Chin is looking for you," Steve said, walking into the study. "Kai is here."

"Quick, hide!" I yelled. I dragged Steve behind one of Mr. Chin's sculptures.

"But . . . ," Steve said, trailing off.

"Shhhh. They'll never find us here," I whispered.

"Ember!" I heard Mr. Chin call. I held my breath.

I was sure we were well hidden. But it turns out I have a very long tail. And Smelly Steve has a very specific smell.

"There you are, Ember!" Mr. Chin said. "It's time to go!"

"You will pay for this, human," I grumbled. But I followed him down the stairs.

Lucy clipped on my leash. "The first day of swim camp, the first day of Kevin's baking internship, *and* the first day of your doggy-playtime group. It's a big day for us Chins," she said, petting my ears. Then she kissed the top of my head. "You'll be great!"

So I had no choice but to go to the dog park and face the greatest threat that Earth has ever seen.

CHAPTER 4

Hyper Space

There were pugs all around me.

Kai held six leashes in one hand, and I had to work hard not to get my leash tangled.

"SNOORT," the pugs all said at once.

The smallest pug, who I'd talked to the day before, walked in front of me. I decided to call her Curly for her extra-curly tail.

There were lots of exciting sights and smells. When we passed a lilac bush, Curly's tail began to wag.

"Flowers!" Curly cried. She ran to sniff them. But she stopped short when she noticed me watching.

"When we invade Earth, these flowers will be taken to our home planet," Curly declared.

"Oh, no, you won't. Those flowers belong here!" I said with as much force as I could muster.

"Too bad. These flowers will be ours!" she said. And then she bit off a lilac flower.

"HOW DARE YOU!" I barked.

But right then, Kai tugged at our leashes. "Come on, everyone. We're here!" he said.

We turned a corner, and there it was—the park! There was green grass as far as I could see, with a fence that kept all the dogs inside.

Kai opened the gate, led us in, and took off our leashes.

I sniffed the ground, avoiding the pugs. Nothing beats the sweet smell of dirt and fresh grass. For a moment, I thought this day might not be *so* bad.

Until suddenly—

"INCOMING!" a voice yelled.

I looked up. Ahead of me, there was a group of dogs running in a pack. It was a STAMPEDE.

And it was hurtling straight toward me!

CHAPTER 5

Unidentified Flying Dogs

*W*HOOSH.

A giant figure ran past me and almost knocked me off my feet.

"NEW FRIENDS!" a voice yelled.

"Yes! Friends!" another voice yelled.

I heard excited barking all around me.

"Hi!"

"Hi!"

"Hi!" the dogs all said.

22

I was surrounded by big dogs that were twice my size. There were so many of them!

"Welcome to the dog park," a fluffy dog said.

"Um, thank you," I said. I tried to sound as big and confident as I could. "I'm Ember, future ruler of—"

"Want to play?" a yellow dog asked.

"Play?" I asked. "I don't play. I plot world domination."

"Sounds fun! Ready, set, GOOO!" a gray dog yelled.

Then they were ZOOMING around me, barking happily.

I was trapped in a dog hurricane!

I cowered against the fence. When I looked back up, the pugs had been swept away in the crowd.

"Hey, let him get settled," Kai said to the big dogs.

"Don't worry, little guy," Kai said, turning to me. "You can play anywhere. We have sticks for fetch, and there are some little dogs in the corner who prefer to stay together. The only rule is no balls—the big dogs get WAY too excited."

"I am not a little guy. I am a fearsome dark overlord," I said, puffing out my chest.

But Kai wasn't listening.

I crept to a corner by the fence. I couldn't see the pugs anywhere, which meant they were probably up to no good.

I thought about the evil alien battles I'd seen in that scary movie.

My ears drooped. I was alone with no friends, up against a galactic evil.

Then I heard a voice. It was maybe the best sound I'd ever heard because it was *familiar*.

"Ember!!" Zar the Russian wolfhound called out.

Zar is an ENORMOUS dog and a good friend. I always feel safer near him! Right away, I knew things were about to get better.

Until I realized he sounded panicked.

"Ember! Where are you?" Zar called again. "Ember, HELLLLP!"

CHAPTER 6

Dog Park: First Contact

I ran toward Zar's voice. He sounded so scared! Was it the pugs?

I skidded to a stop. Zar was cornered! All around him were . . . the *smallest* dogs I've ever seen.

27

One was a poodle who came up to Zar's ankle. Another one looked like a tiny mop. Then there was a dog who was long and very low to the ground.

They formed a ring around Zar and sniffed at him curiously.

"Save me, Ember!" he called.

"Hey! Don't hurt my friend!" I barked, leaping between the small dogs and Zar.

"We don't bite! We just wanted to say hello," the long dog said.

"Oh," Zar said, relaxing a little. "Sorry. You all made me nervous."

"It's okay. We were scared on our first day at the dog park, too," the long dog replied. "My name is Tomato."

"I'm Scone," the poodle said.

"And I'm King," the mop dog said in a high squeaky voice.

"Want to play?" Tomato asked.

"Well . . . ," Zar said. I could tell he wasn't sure, so I needed to think fast.

"Uh, no, thanks. We're good! Right, Zar?" I asked, hoping he would take my cue.

"Uh, right, Ember," Zar said, sounding a bit uncertain.

Deep down, I was relieved. Now I wouldn't have to worry about making friends. And I had Zar all to myself.

"Well, if you change your mind, you know where to find us," Tomato said.

Then the small dogs walked off.

"This park is overwhelming," Zar said. "Today is my first day."

"Mine too," I said. "I'm glad to see you."

"Yeah, together, there's nothing to be nervous about—" Zar began.

"Yes, now that I am here, we can face an untold evil together," I said.

"Wait, what UNTOLD EVIL?!" Zar screeched. Zar is scared of a lot of things.

"The pugs in this dog park are *aliens*," I whispered in a low voice.

"Wait, aliens are real?!" Zar asked.

"Yes, and they're plotting to invade our planet! That can only mean one thing," I explained.

"What?" he asked.

"It's up to us to save the world!" I said.

CHAPTER 7

The Pug
Strikes Back

Where are the pugs? I wondered. Zar and I had searched the dog park, and there was no sign of them. And Zar was VERY tall, so he could see everywhere.

Except one spot—

"Hey, what's over there?" I asked.

In the far corner, by the fence, was a shed.

"Oh, that's where they store supplies for our doggy-playtime group," Zar

said. "I heard the humans talking about it."

"That must be where the pugs are hiding," I said. "Come on!"

We trotted over.

Kai and the other humans were close by, talking and watching the big dogs run.

"Let's sneak around the back," I whispered to Zar. "Be very quiet."

We tiptoed around the shed. It was a little easier for me than Zar, since his paws are the size of my head. But he did a great job.

As we got closer, I saw a hole in the wall. The hole was wide enough for a small dog, like a pug, to fit through.

"This must be how they got inside," I whispered.

Zar and I peered in.

For a moment, we just saw shadows.

Then, as my eyes got used to the dark, I saw lots of moving shapes.

The pugs were *building* something. It towered high above them. I could make out wheels, a ramp, and a big oval shape on top.

"Is it an evil space laser?" Zar whispered, his voice shaking.

"No," I whispered in horror. "It's a SHIP."
The pugs were building a real *spaceship*.
Right then, a sinister evil sound echoed behind me.
"SNOOOOORT."
I whirled around.
We were surrounded again—this time, by pugs!

CHAPTER 8

Not the Dogs You're Looking For

You two shouldn't be looking in there," a pug warned as Zar and I jumped around.

More pugs spilled out from the shed. How would we get around them all?

I panicked as the pugs closed in. But then a loud voice rang out—"SNEAK ATTACK! RUN!"

I saw a strange shape with two long ears charging forward. The shape was small, but it was surprising enough that the pugs leapt back.

That's when Zar and I burst past the pugs. We didn't stop running until we were safely across the dog park. Our rescuer was following right behind us.

We collapsed in a heap on the grass.

"Thank you, stranger. You saved us!" I said.

"Of course! Anytime, Ember!" a familiar voice answered.

Our rescuer was . . . Steve!

But Steve looked different. He had a big black button tied over his nose with a piece of Lucy's hair ribbons. Two old, dirty socks were attached to his ears with paper clips.

"I'm in disguise and undercover . . . as a dog!" he said proudly.

"Umm." Zar and I looked at each other. Steve didn't look like any dog I'd seen before. But I

didn't want to hurt his feelings.

"Great job," I said.

"So convincing," Zar agreed.

"I came up with my costume this morning. I wanted to see how your day at the dog park was going! And Neo helped me get here safely. She's up in that tree keeping an eye on things!" Steve said.

I looked up and waved a paw.

"Hi, Ember!" Neo sang from a tree branch.

"This place is AMAZING," Steve said.

"Well, it's nicer now that you're here. But we can't get distracted. We must stop the evil pugs!" I cried.

"Yeah, but what were they building?" Zar asked. "It looked HUGE, and scar—"

"Hey, is that a sock?" a voice behind Steve interrupted.

A big dog came up and sniffed Steve's fake ear.

"Uhhh," Steve said.

"I love socks! Let's play!" the dog said.

Before we could get away, the dog grabbed one of Steve's fake sock ears and dragged Steve along with him!

"Steeeeve!" I yelled as my friend flew across the park.

"Oh no!" Zar yelled.

"WHEEEE!" Steve yelled. "I LOVE THE DOG PARK!"

To my surprise, Steve was having fun! *And* he was making new friends!

It was official.

I HATED the dog park.

CHAPTER 9

Total Eclipse of the Tarts

I watched Steve and the big dogs play for a while, until they were too dizzy to play more.

"Great game, Steve!" a striped dog said.

"Yeah, see you tomorrow!" Steve replied with a big smile.

I felt a strange droop in my tail. Steve was making new friends at the park without me!

Just then, Kai called my name.

"Ember, time to go home!"

Steve snuck away just as Kai came over with leashes. I could see Neo in the sky, flying away with Steve.

Kai led the pugs and me out of the park.

The pugs glared at me as we walked. I looked at the ground and pretended they weren't there.

When we reached my house, I ran up the stairs. I was so happy to be home! I knew that here, I'd be okay. I still didn't know how to stop the pugs, but my friends and I would figure out what to do.

That's when the front door opened, and Neo came flying down the hallway. Steve was close by, his disguise gone.

"Ember! Lucy and Kevin have a problem!" Steve said.

So I ran out to where they were sitting in the living room. Both of them looked sad, and Kevin was slumped against the couch.

"Next week, there's a bake sale at the science museum," Kevin said. "I have to make space-themed jam tarts, but I'm so bad at it!" Kevin was taking baking classes this summer, while Lucy was at swim camp.

"Arjun and Lia are making new friends already," Lucy began. "I thought it would be the three of us all summer. Maya, Arjun's new friend, is an AMAZING swimmer. And Hanai, Lia's new friend, makes up the best water games. I'll never be as cool as they are!"

Lucy sighed.

I was proud of Lucy and Kevin for being honest about their feelings and for sharing them with each other. But still, I didn't want them to be sad.

So I jumped up on the couch and put my nose in Lucy's ear. Steve rolled around in his ball at Kevin's feet.

But neither of them laughed.

And Lucy and Kevin were in bad moods all afternoon and at dinner. Steve, Neo, and I were too busy trying to cheer them up to talk more about the evil pugs.

"Don't worry, Lucy," I said as we got into bed. "Everything will be okay."

But I'd spoken too soon.

I was drifting off to sleep when I heard a loud "SNOORT."

I jumped up. The room was quiet. Was it just a dream?

But then it came again.

"Snoooort."

I crept to Lucy's window. Outside, I could just make out something in the backyard.

A shadowy figure with a curly tail was looking straight at me.

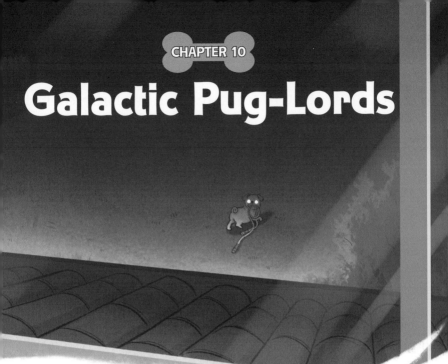

CHAPTER 10
Galactic Pug-Lords

Ahhh!" I barked at the pug as loud as I could.

"Ember?" Lucy mumbled with her eyes closed.

I stopped barking and turned back to the window. The pug had something in its mouth. It looked like Lucy's old jump rope from the backyard. But I couldn't be sure, and soon, the pug was gone.

I tiptoed back to my pillow. We were safe for now, but it took me a long time to fall asleep again.

The next morning, I told Steve and Neo what I'd seen.

"The alien pugs were in our backyard at night?!" Neo said.

"This is serious!" Steve said. "You need help today. I'll come to the park again. I can be in disguise as a rock this time. Or grass! Or—"

"Steve, NO. The dog park is for dogs!" I yelled. I didn't mean to say it like that. It just came out. Because what if Steve made more friends at the park? And what if he liked those friends more than *me*?

Steve looked sad.

Just then, Kai knocked at the front door.

I left the house with my tail drooping. And the pugs were waiting for me.

"Remember, do not get in our way or you'll be sorry," one of them said.

I turned to Curly.

"It's YOU who will be sorry," I said. "I will find a way to stop you!"

"Do not interfere, Earthling. All will be revealed," Curly said.

I stayed as far away as I could for the rest of the walk.

When we got to the park, the pugs went straight to their shed. I shivered, imagining the work they were doing on their spaceship.

Zar was already there. He was talking with Tomato and the smaller dogs.

"Hi, Ember!" Zar said. "I've just been talking to Tomato and Scone! They like playing hide-and-go-seek, just like I do! We should play with them later."

"No! I mean, uh, I don't think we can trust them. They might be in on the pugs' evil plan," I whispered.

"Really? But they don't talk to the pugs at all," Zar said.

"Trust me," I replied. "They're not on our side."

"Hmm, okay," Zar said. His tail drooped.

We walked to another corner of the park. Tomato was frowning and looking at me. She'd heard what I'd said to Zar, and it looked like her feelings were hurt.

I didn't know what to do.

So I decided I'd play hide-and-seek with Zar. But before we knew it, Zar's human came to pick him up early for a vet appointment.

I watched him

go. There was no way I could defeat the pugs alone. And now all the other dogs knew I didn't want to play with them, too.

I put my head on my paws. Things couldn't get any worse.

That is, until suddenly, the entire sun was blocked out.

Guiding Stars

Something huge was standing over me, blocking the sun!

It was . . . Tomato?

"Hi, Ember," Tomato said.

I jumped to my feet. I realized that Tomato wasn't suddenly a giant. She just looked much taller when I was lying at her feet.

"Do you want some company?" she asked.

"Really? Even when I said I didn't want to play?" I asked. "Why are you being nice to me when I was so mean to you?"

"Oh, I was the same way when I first got here," Tomato said. "I know the dog park can be a scary place. It can be easier to be alone, so you don't have to worry about making friends. Of course, if you DO want to be alone, I respect that. But if you want company, I'd love to be your friend."

"Wow," I said. "Tomato, you are a wise dog! When I rule the world, you will be one of my chief advisers."

"Great!" Tomato said with a grin. "Now, want to play?"

And I did.

I spent the rest of the afternoon with Tomato, Scone, and King. Scone taught me how to stand on my two back legs and spin. King was EXCELLENT at jumping. And Tomato answered all the questions I had about the dog park.

"Thank you, new friends," I said, when it was time to go home. "You will be rewarded. And I will keep you safe from harm, I promise."

"Thanks, new guy!" King said in his squeaky voice.

"See you tomorrow, Ember," Tomato said.

I smiled and trotted toward Kai. The pugs were getting their leashes on. I still didn't know how I was going to stop them. But I finally knew where to start.

CHAPTER 12

A New Hope

$\mathbf{I}$ raced into the house.

"Neo, I need everyone's help!" I cried.

So Neo, who is an amazing friend, assembled Zar and Steve in the yard.

"I'm sorry!" I blurted out right away. "I was scared you'd both make new friends at the dog park. That's why I tried to stop you from having fun or meeting new pets. I shouldn't have done that."

"Aw, thanks so much, Ember!" Zar said. "I understand. I was scared, too!"

I looked to Steve. He was unusually quiet. Was he still mad at me?

And then—

"I'm SORRY, TOOOOO!" Steve said. He ran over and gave me a hug that almost knocked me to the ground.

"I was scared YOU'D make new friends who you liked more than me!" Steve cried, hugging me tightly. "That's why I went to the dog park in the first place."

"I would be honored to have you at the dog park, loyal hamster," I said.

I had so much more to say. But just then, we heard voices in the driveway. Lucy and Kevin were home!

So Zar raced back to his own yard, and Neo, Steve, and I went inside to greet them.

Lucy and Kevin dropped their bags and headed straight for the kitchen.

"Jam tart practice time!" Kevin declared.

"And I'm your taste tester!" Lucy said. She patted my head while Kevin set out his ingredients.

"Was swim camp better today?" Kevin asked.

"Yeah," Lucy said. "I'm getting used to things. Though I don't know if Maya and Hanai like me. I'm inviting them to have a picnic in two days at the park. I'm a little nervous about it."

"Maybe things will change when you get to know each other," Kevin said.

"Hmmmm," Lucy said.

They were quiet for a minute.

Then, Lucy turned to Kevin, with a big smile. "You're a good big brother," she said. "Also, you have something on your face."

She reached out and wiped a big smear of jam onto his nose.

"Hey!" Kevin said, laughing. Then he turned to the counter and grabbed the jar. "JAM FIGHT!" he yelled, and they began flicking jam at each other.

"Amazing! Try some, Ember!" Steve said as some jam fell on the kitchen floor. "It's DELICIOUS."

"Soon we'll both be purple," Lucy said, laughing and licking jam from her fingers.

Suddenly, I had an idea!

"STEVE!" I turned to my loyal hamster, who also would soon be purple. "YOU HAD THE KEY TO OUR PLAN ALL ALONG!"

CHAPTER 13

The Final Countdown

Neo, Steve, and I raced upstairs to Mr. Chin's office.

"We're going to steal the spaceship from the pugs!" I said. "And Steve is the key!"

Steve puffed out his chest proudly as I explained my plan. It would involve our new dog-park friends and a LOT of jam.

66

Mr. Chin wasn't happy about the huge mess we made all over the house. While we tried to help Mr. Chin clean, Neo flew out to tell Zar the plan. I was almost too excited to sleep that night.

The next morning, I was waiting for Kai at the door.

It was time to put our plan in motion.

Since Zar gets to the park first every day, it was his job to tell Tomato, Scone, and King the details. As Kai led us into the park, I spotted my friends getting into position.

Neo fluttered into the trees, where the humans couldn't see her.

I held my breath as I waited for the signal.

And then—there it was!

Slowly, a soccer ball rolled into the center of the dog park.

It was rolling all by itself.

But it wasn't magic. It was . . . Steve!

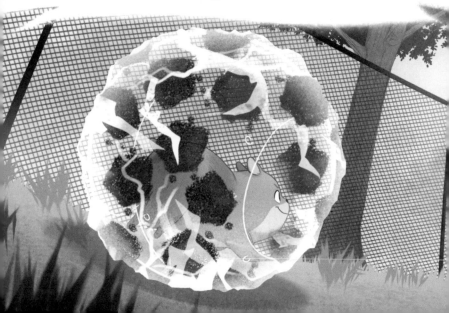

We had painted Steve's ball with jam and flour, wrapped it in plastic wrap, and poked two holes for air. And now, as he rolled into the center of the park, all the big dogs froze.

"Ball!" one of them barked.

"Hey, no balls allowed!" Kai called. But it was too late.

The big dogs began running toward the ball.

"WHEEEEEEE!" Steve called. He sped around the park, and the dogs ran to chase him.

It was CHAOS. I could see the pugs against the fence. Tomato and the small dogs were in a ring around them, barking to keep them there. The humans didn't notice—they were too busy trying to get to the Steve-ball.

In the confusion, Zar and I ran back to the shed while Neo flew behind us. All we had to do was figure out how to steal the spaceship, or take it apart.

"AHA!" I cried as I raced in through the hole in the shed.

But then I froze.

The pugs had done more work, and we now saw exactly what they were building.

It WAS a ship.

But it wasn't for outer space.

CHAPTER 14

The Truth Is Out There

What is THAT?" Neo said with a gasp.

"I'm not sure," I said. We crept closer to the pugs' ship. But suddenly—

BAM! The pugs burst into the shed.

Tomato, Scone, and King were right behind them, along with Steve.

"THIS IS THE BEST DAY EVER!" Steve said, before collapsing in a dizzy heap.

"Sorry, Ember, the pugs got past us!" Tomato said.

We turned to face the pugs, but they didn't look scary. They looked *worried*.

"We're almost finished! Don't harm our ship!" Curly yelled.

"Shh, don't tell them our plan, Ravioli!" one of the other pugs said.

"Quiet, Ziti!" another pug said.

"Don't tell me what to do, Spaghettio!"

Then they were all talking over one another.

"Wait, what's going on?!" I demanded.

"I'll explain," said the pug I'd been calling Curly. "My name is Ravioli. And these are my brothers and sisters: Ziti, Fusilli, Spaghettio, and Macaroni."

The pugs snorted hello as they were introduced.

"This is our ship," Ravioli said.

"For world domination?" I gasped.

"No, it's an old wagon! We found it in the shed, and we've been trying to fix it, and to build a harness so we can pull it. It's for our neighbor, Melon," Ravioli said.

"She hurt her paw," Spaghettio added.

"She can't walk to the park," Fusilli said.

"She's been feeling very left out," Ziti chimed in.

"So if we pull her in the wagon, she'll be with us!" Macaroni finished.

"Only we've failed," Ravioli said sadly. "The wagon is too heavy."

"But . . . ," I said. I was confused. "But you said you were aliens! You said the planet would be yours!"

"I know. I'm sorry about that," Ravioli said. "It started as a joke."

"We thought it would make us stand out," Ziti added.

"So you'd like us!" Fusilli cried.

"But then we realized it made other dogs scared of us," Macaroni said.

"Which isn't what we wanted!" Ziti said.

"But we were just so nervous about the dog park. We thought no one would be mean to us if they were scared of us," Spaghettio added.

"Sorry," Fusilli said. "We come in peace and want to be friends."

"We just want the park to be for all of us. Including our friend Melon," Ravioli said.

I couldn't believe it. The pugs weren't evil after all! And now I had even more friends to help me someday rule the world.

"Yes, the park SHOULD be for all of us," I declared. I turned to Zar. "And this time, YOU are the key, Zar. And I promise, it won't be scary at all."

"YAY!" Zar barked.

"But first," Steve said. "How about a game of ball tag?!"

My tail wagged faster than it had in days.

CHAPTER 15

Rocket Dog

That afternoon, we played lots of games.

Zar, Tomato, Scone, Macaroni, and Ziti played hide-and-seek.

Ravioli, King, and I raced.

Steve, Fusilli, and Spaghettio played with the big dogs. Fusilli could jump almost as high as Zar's tail. We cheered her on with happy barks.

"See?" Kai said, when it was time to go home. "I *knew* you'd like the dog park."

"Thank you, human," I said. "You will be rewarded."

"Goodbye, Ravioli, Ziti, Fusilli, Spaghettio, and Macaroni!" I said when we got to my house. "See you tomorrow!"

All our tails wagged excitedly.

Lucy opened the door and unclipped my leash.

"Tomorrow's the picnic! I can't wait to see where you play at the park," Lucy said. She patted my head.

"When I rule the world, every day will be a picnic!" I cried.

After dinner and our walk, it was time for bed. I was almost too excited to sleep. Luckily, before I knew it, it was the next day.

Lucy put my leash on and grabbed a bag of almond cookies and a picnic blanket. Then we walked to the dog park together.

Arjun and Lia were waiting for us, along with Izzy, Arjun's dog. Just as we finished setting up, our new friends arrived.

I watched with pride as the pugs marched in with their human. Behind them came Zar. He was pulling the wagon, using Lucy's old jump rope. The wagon was decorated with flowers, which I knew was thanks to Ravioli aka Curly. In the wagon, there was a snow-white dog with a cast on her paw who had to be Melon!

Behind them was another dog and human.

"Hi Hanai!" Lucy called.

"Hi everyone!" the human holding all the pugs's leashes said. She seemed very nice.

"Hi, Maya!" Arjun called. The other human waved.

Tomato was running next to the wagon.

"Hi, Ember!" Tomato said. "This is Maya, my human. She's great!"

The humans spread out their picnic, and I went to greet my fellow pets.

My tail wagged proudly as Lucy sat down next to Hanai and Maya.

"I'm so glad you're both here," she said with a shy smile.

"Of course, thank you for inviting us," Maya said.

"I'm so glad we can hang out!" Hanai said. "I love the games you make up in in the pool!"

"No way! I love the games *you* make up!" Lucy said.

And then they were all talking and laughing, like they'd been friends forever. Soon, Arjun and Lia joined in.

I watched them happily. I was learning that new friends are nothing to be scared of. In fact, it turns out you can never have too many friends! I liked that idea a lot.

And speaking of friends . . .

"Ember!" another familiar voice called. It was Steve!

Kevin was carrying him toward us. In his other hand, Kevin had a basket.

"Guess what we brought," Steve said. "I'll give you a hint: they're out of this world!"

CHAPTER 16

Space Jam (and Real Jam) Are GREAT

It took practice, but I finally figured out the recipe! They're PERFECT!" Kevin said. He held up a bag of golden, rocket-shaped jam tarts.

"Yay!" everyone cheered.

Then there was a lot of eating, running in the grass, and watching the pugs and Zar play fetch with Steve's ball.

Mr. and Mrs. Chin, Arjun's dads, and Lia's mom and dad, joined us soon after that. They brought even more food, and were smiling like they had a surprise.

"Guess what. We have great news!" cried Dr. Ramanathan, Arjun's dad. "Arjun, Lia, Lucy, we're going on a trip with all our families!"

"Oh wow!" Lucy said.

"That's so cool!" Arjun cheered.

"Yay!" Lia said.

"Some of the pets will stay with a sitter, but Izzy, Ember, and Sweet Pea will come along," Mr. Chin said. "You'll love it. We're going to Acorn Island."

"Is that a new kingdom?!" I asked. My ears perked up. At last! This was a chance to take over new parts of the world!

But the other pets GASPED.

"I've heard of Acorn Island," Ravioli said. She looked worried.

"Oh, is it nice?" Steve asked.

"No, it's not nice," Ziti said with big eyes. "The woods on Acorn Island are HAUNTED."

"What?!" I asked. "What do you mean?"

"They're haunted by a mysterious evil," Macaroni whispered.

"Yes," Fusilli said. "Everyone says the evil chipmunk walks at night! And she sees all!"

Susan Tan lives in Cambridge, Massachusetts. She grew up with lots of small dogs who all could rule the world. Susan is the author of the Cilla Lee-Jenkins series, and *Ghosts, Toast, and Other Hazards*. She enjoys knitting, crocheting, and petting every dog who will let her. Pets Rule! is her first early chapter book series.

Wendy Tan Shiau Wei is a Chinese-Malaysian illustrator based in Kuala Lumpur, Malaysia. Over the last few years, she has contributed to numerous animation productions and advertisements. Now her passion for storytelling has led her down a new path: illustrating children's books. When she's not drawing, Wendy likes to spend time playing with her mix-breed rescue dog, Lucky. The love for her dog is her inspiration to help this book come to life!

Pets RULE!

Invasion of the Pugs

Questions & Activities

Ember is not excited to go to a new doggy playtime group. Why does he ask Bubbles, the pet goldfish, to hide him in Mr. Chin's office?

Ember is relieved to see his friend Zar at the park. On page 26, why does Zar yell for help?

 Ember thinks the pugs have an evil plan to take over the earth. What do Ember and Zar see when they peek into the shed?

Ember's friend Steve shows up to the park in a special disguise. What is his costume made of?

Ember thinks the pugs are aliens from outer space. Draw and label a picture of your own spaceship!